Squishy Taylor

Squishy Taylor is published by
Picture Window Books,
A Capstone Imprint
1710 Roe Crest Drive
North Mankato, Minnesota 56003
www.mycapstone.com

Squishy Taylor and the Bonus Sisters
Text copyright © 2016 Ailsa Wild
Illustration copyright © 2016 Ben Wood
Series design copyright © 2016 Hardie Grant Egmont
First published in Australia by Hardie Grant Egmont 2016

Published in American English in 2018 by Picture Window Books

Library of Congress Cataloging-in-Publication Data is
is on file with the Library of Congress.

ISBN: 978-1-5158-1972-1 (paperback)
ISBN: 978-1-5158-1976-9 (reflowable epub)

Summary: Squishy Taylor and her dad have just moved in with the
two most annoying twin sisters EVER. But when Squishy finds a
runaway boy hiding in their basement, she'll need all the help
she can get!

Printed in China.
010735S18

and the
Bonus Sisters

Ailsa Wild
with art by BEN WOOD

PICTURE WINDOW BOOKS
a capstone imprint

For Toby and Emily and
their wild bonus family.
— Ailsa

For Jess, my new bonus sister.
— Ben

Chapter One

Baby is on the changing table, poopy and kicking. Dad looks flustered. "Please, Squishy," he asks me, "can you get the baby wipes? They're in the car."

Squishy Taylor to the rescue.

I turn and grab the car key, ducking out our front door to pause in the hallway. Elevator or stairs? **Which is more fun?** Stairs, of course — all eleven flights of them. I bolt past the other apartments

to the stairwell, then leap down the steps
like a **ninja-gazelle**.

I slow
down at the
bottom before
I get to the
garage. It's always
been a bit dark and creepy down here.

Our car is at the far end, with the other cars from the eleventh floor. To get there I have to pass under a flickering light that's more off than on.

That's when I hear the noise. A kind of rustling, scuttling noise — but big, way bigger than a rat. I stand still and listen, with my heart all **racy-fast**. The noise is near our car. I take a deep breath and tiptoe down the last five steps and out into the garage.

The fluorescent light **buzzes** and flickers off, and then I'm walking through the dark. There's that rustle again. I freeze. By now I'm closer to the car than I am to the steps. I make a **bolt** for it, pressing the unlock button so the car beeps and flashes just before I get to it. I pull open the back door, scramble over Baby's car seat, and slam the door behind me.

I'm sitting on the baby wipes, listening to myself breathing. Whatever was out there knows I'm here.

A movement from a few cars away catches my eye. A dark, shadowy, **dodging** movement. Like someone trying to hide. It reminds me of something. There it is again, ducking away behind another car. I realize what it reminds me of: myself, sneaking through the garage just now.

I watch. The flickering light comes on again, and then I see the person running. I grin. It's definitely a little kid, a boy darting away from me.

For some reason, that makes me want to chase him. I jump out of the car, and the kid **bolts**. I run between the cars. There's the sound of a door closing and then nothing.

I look around. "Hey! Where'd you go? Come out!" I call.

Nothing. **Jeepers**, this kid must be scared.

"My name is Squishy Taylor," I shout. "I'm not going to hurt you."

After another silence, a door I hadn't noticed creaks open and a voice says, "What kind of a name is Squishy?"

I can see boy's sunburned face and dirty sweater.

"It's a good kind of name," I say. "A special name."

Mom and Dad gave me the nickname when I was little, because I used to squeeze between them when they were hugging. I'd wriggle myself in, yelling, "Squish me! Squish me!" They got divorced a long time ago, but they both still call me Squishy.

I feel lucky, because I'm sure no one else in the world is named Squishy.

The boy is in a storage room, which I've never seen before. As he steps out, I get a glimpse over his shoulder of a backpack and a sleeping bag laid out neatly on the floor. He pulls the door closed behind him.

"What are you doing here?" I ask.

"Nothing," he says.

"That's not true," I say.

"Well," he says, shrugging, "your real name's not Squishy."

It's not. It's Sita, after my grandma, but that's only for **serious-in-trouble** times. This boy doesn't need to know all about that.

We stare at each other.

"Do you have any food?" he asks.

"Well, dinner's almost ready," I say, but I know that's not what he means. He looks so sad that I feel sorry for him. "You want me to sneak you some later?"

He nods hard.

"How about we make a deal? I bring you food, and then you tell me what you're doing here."

He looks torn, then says, "Only if you promise not to tell **anyone**."

I grin. "Course!" I say. "You're the best kind of secret there is."

Just then, I remember something. I run to our car and grab a package of crackers (and the wipes) from the back seat.

I hand the food over. "I'll have to wait until Dad and Alice and Baby are asleep before I sneak out, but these should keep you going."

The boy grins. "Thanks, Squishy Taylor," he says.

"See you in the middle of the night!" I say as I run for the elevator.

It's not until I'm at our apartment door that I realize I never asked his name.

Chapter Two

All through dinner, I'm burning with my secret.

Jessie and Vee aren't talking to me, but I don't care anymore. They sit down at the table at the same time, flicking their **twin ponytails** at the same time, scowling their **twin scowls**. Their mom, Alice, plonks plates of spaghetti onto the table while Dad gets glasses of water.

Baby pounds the table with his fat arms, drops broccoli on the floor, and shouts.

This is what normal looks like now. I used to live with Mom, and Dad lived by himself. Then Dad moved here when he and Alice had Baby. When Mom got her job in Geneva, Switzerland, we decided I should move in with Dad and Alice too. So now I've lived here seven and a half weeks, and it's the official new "normal."

Dad told me that stepfamilies get a bad rap in fairy tales and maybe I should think of them as a "bonus family" instead. I don't think they're a bonus. They are about ninety-five percent annoying and five percent really, really annoying.

But tonight I don't care because I've got a secret.

I suck spaghetti strands and smile at my fork.

After dinner, I grab the iPad before Jessie can. She scowls but says nothing. The only time I don't have to fight for the iPad is when it's time to Skype Mom. I lie on my tummy on the floor and push my curls out of my face.

"Hi, **Squishy-sweet**," Mom says.

"Hi, Mom."

"Let me just finish this sentence." She starts typing. Mom's at work because it's daytime in Geneva. She finishes with a swing of her arm, then looks at me again. "What did you do today?" she asks.

"Um . . ." The first thing I think of is the boy downstairs, but if I told her about him she'd probably tell Dad. "Um . . . I poured orange juice and flour in Vee's backpack this morning," I say.

She groans. "Oh, great. Poor Vee." But she has her sideways smile on. Mom was a rebel as a kid, so she kind of likes that I am too.

"You should have seen the **goop** it made," I add, thinking gleefully of the dough all over her pencil case. "It was all . . . **squishy!**"

She laughs. "That's probably not the best way to make friends with your stepsister, huh?"

"I don't want to be *friends*! I've got friends at school. Did you know, Jessie spent an hour yesterday telling me how to do my homework —"

Just then, Jessie comes in and looks over my shoulder at Mom. "Hi, Devika," she says.

"Hi, Jessie," Mom says.

"How's the United Nations?" Jessie asks as if she's **one hundred years older** than me — not five and a half months.

"Oh," Mom sighs. "Lots of paperwork. Huge. I don't know."

Jessie waves at Mom and heads over to her telescope by the window.

"Well, how *are* your school friends?" Mom asks me with a smile. "I bet they're all wishing you would get on a plane to Geneva."

I grin. My school friends are one of the main reasons I stayed. "Nah. They're good." But I don't really want to talk to her in front of Jessie. "Love you," I say.

"Love you too, Squish," Mom says, and her picture slides away.

"Bedtime in seven minutes!" Alice yells.

Vee runs into the room and does a **kicking-two-jump-scramble** up to the top bunk. She's such a show-off. Vee always invents new ways of getting to the top bunk and then performs them like we should clap. When I try them, she does **bigger-kid-snob face** at me and pretends she's better. Which makes it way less fun.

Jessie takes the iPad from me without asking. She checks her telescope and makes notes in her astronomy app. Then she folds her clothes into a neat square and slips into the bottom bunk.

"Goodnight, Vee," Jessie says.

"Goodnight, Jessie," Vee says.

They don't say anything to me. Which is kind of fair enough, since I made that **fabulous mess** in Vee's bag this morning. But that was fair enough, because Vee drew a mustache on my face with permanent marker while I was asleep last night. I got it scrubbed off before school, but I had a red upper lip until recess.

Anyway. Whatever. I climb into the middle bunk in the stupid **triple bunk**

bed Alice built for the three of us before I moved in — right in between the twin-generated-silence.

Time passes, but I make myself stay awake. I wait, thinking about my secret.

After a long time, the line of light under our door goes out. I hear Dad and Alice's bedroom door close. Jessie and Vee are both doing sleep-breathing.

I slowly peel back the covers and tiptoe into the kitchen. It looks as though Dad or Alice discovered the **secret stash** of garlic bread and meatballs I hid under the table earlier, but it's fine, the stash is just sitting in the top part of the trash can. I grab an old plastic container and pile them in. Then I lift the key off of the hook and ease open the front door.

When I get out into the hall, I realize I don't just have to hide from Dad and Alice. I have to hide from every single adult in the building. Grown-ups take the responsibility of being grown-ups very seriously. Especially if they see kids wearing pajamas out in the middle of the night.

Luckily, no one spots me and I make it into the garage just fine. I tap on the storage-room door. "Roomservice," I say.

As the boy opens up, I hear the garage door begin to beep and rise. Headlights shine into the garage. He stumbles backward, and I follow him in, closing the door behind us.

"Thanks," he says as I hand him the food. "Hope they didn't notice the light."

He shoves a meatball into his mouth, and we listen to the car pull up. We sit on his sleeping bag with our backs to the wall.

"What's your name?" I ask.

"John," he says, with his mouth full. "John Smith."

"Why are you here?" I ask.

"I'm hiding," he says, taking a bite of garlic bread.

"No way!" I say sarcastically.

"From the police."

I stop being sarcastic and make a **question-face** instead.

"I stole a motorcycle," he says. "When the driver got off, I jumped on and drove it all the way across town. Now they want to put me in prison."

"They don't put kids in prison," I say.

I think for a little bit.

"Next time I come to see you, I'll do a secret knock, OK?" I say. "Don't open to anyone except me."

"OK," he says. "What will it sound like?"

I make up a really complicated knock that nobody else would *ever* do.

He shakes his head. "I didn't get that. Do it again?" he asks.

But I can't remember it. I make up another one, but then I can't remember that either. It makes us both laugh. Finally we agree on a pretty quick and simple tappety-tap-tap-tap.

I stand up.

"Don't tell anyone I'm here," he says.

"Of course not," I say.

"Will you bring food tomorrow night?" he asks. He suddenly sounds lonely.

"I will bring you **so much food**," I tell him as I grin.

But when I open the door to leave, Vee is standing on the other side.

Chapter Three

"What are you *doing*?" Vee hisses.

John Smith is hiding behind me, but he's pretty obvious. There's no point pretending.

"John Smith, this is my stepsister, Vee. Vee, this is John. He stole a motorcycle and is hiding from the police."

"You did not steal a motorcycle," Vee says, but she sounds fascinated by the whole story.

John nods.

"I'm looking after him here," I declare, "and I've promised to protect him with my life."

I know that's not exactly what I promised, but John doesn't seem to mind. Vee looks a tiny bit impressed.

"I'll protect him too," she says.

I want to say no and keep John Smith all to myself. I start to shake my head.

"With my life," Vee adds, sticking her chin out.

I figure if she's not with me, she's against me. "You can help protect him," I say slowly. "But you're not allowed to tell Jessie. She will tell the police for sure."

John looks worried. "Please don't tell," he says.

Vee looks unsure, but I make her put one hand on her heart and the other hand on John's shoulder. I tell her to look deep into his eyes and promise to protect him. I realize John really should have made me do this, so I do it too.

There's something very serious about it. Suddenly I care even more that John doesn't get discovered.

Then we tell John we'll see him tomorrow and start for the elevator.

"On Allowance Day, let's buy him gummy worms," Vee says as the elevator starts climbing. Her voice sounds conspiring, like we're a team. It's kind of surprising and nice.

"Do you think we can sneak in before school?" I ask. "The garage will be busy."

"One of us can be the decoy, while the other sneaks into John's room," Vee says. "What kind of decoy trick could we do?"

"Maybe we can set off the fire alarm," I suggest.

Vee laughs. "Maybe you can pretend to go crazy and sing opera and make everyone look at you."

We make up lots of other stupid decoy tricks. Vee has never been this fun, **ever**. We are giggling so hard when we get to our floor that we totally forget to be quiet.

We would have remembered by the time we got to our door. But we have to go past Mr. Hinkenbushel's first.

His door opens with a bang against the wall. "What are you kids doing up at this time of night?" He's wearing old pajamas, and his face is red. "You're keeping the whole building awake. What are your parents *thinking*?"

When he says "parents," a little spit comes out of his mouth and flies across the hallway. I dodge it like a ninja, but that just makes him angrier.

"Where's your respect?" he shouts.

"Sorry, Mr. Hinkenbushel, sorry," Vee says, and we duck away toward our place. He glares at us as I turn the key, and then we're in. We close the door and lean against it, whisper-giggling. Vee's shoulder is warm, shaking against mine.

"How did you find me?" I ask.

"Not a problem," Vee says. "I was right behind you from the minute you left the bedroom."

"You are so creepy!" I say. We burst into more giggles.

A door creaks open. Dad's sleepy voice breaks in on our laughter. "What are you doing?"

Chapter Four

While we make breakfast, Vee and I bump each other's shoulders and giggle. We're both trying to sneak food for John Smith, but there are too many people watching. Jessie is suspicious. She starts glancing sideways at me as she eats her cereal.

Alice is in the shower getting ready for work, and Dad's trying to **bounce** Baby on his hip and make lunches at the same time. Baby is crying, squirming backward, and hitting Dad in the face with his fat little arm.

"Hey, Tom, how about I do that?" Vee says helpfully, taking the knife from Dad to spread mayo on the sandwiches.

Jessie stares at her like she's suddenly turned into a fake plastic fern. We never make our own lunches.

"Don't think you can wriggle out of your punishment for last night's **shenanigans**," Dad says, but he sounds relieved and bounces Baby over to the other side of the room.

"Oh no, that's fine!" Vee says. I can see that she's **sneakily** making a fourth sandwich.

Last night, we managed to convince Dad we'd only sneaked out as far as the kitchen for snacks. He was so happy I was getting along with Vee that he couldn't pretend to be angry for long. The lie should work as long as Mr. Hinkenbushel doesn't tell. He probably won't. He doesn't like talking to adults. He only likes shouting at kids.

I had the seriously **genius** idea for our punishment.

"We're looking forward to cleaning the car after school," I say brightly. We will have hours to sneak in and out of John's room, bring him food, and ask him questions.

Jessie makes **cross-eyes** at me.

I realize I shouldn't look so happy. But it's too late.

"Maybe I can help you," Jessie says sweetly.

Vee and I glance hopelessly at each other and then realize Jessie is watching us. We're giving ourselves away.

"That sounds great," I say in a matching **fake-nice voice.**

Meanwhile, Baby has started pulling Dad's hair with tiny, white-knuckled fists.

Dad and Baby walk us to the bus stop. There's a tall, scowly man in a neat blue coat standing there. He looks familiar, but I can't tell why. Then I realize I'm staring, so I look away.

"Bye, Dad," I say, as the bus pulls up.

"Bye, Tom," say my stepsisters.

"Be good," Dad says.

"And if you can't be good, be careful!" I call from the bus steps. It's something Mom used to say, and it always makes me laugh.

"*What* is going *on*?" Jessie asks as soon as the bus doors close.

"Nothing," Vee and I say together.

"Don't lie," Jessie says.

"It's nothing," Vee insists.

"We just got up together for leftovers last night," I say, sounding innocent and nice, but really I'm rubbing it in. There's something fun about having Vee on my side for once.

"What, and now you're suddenly best buddies and you want to clean the car together? You might as well pretend you got a job as an **astronaut.** I'm so onto you." Jessie yanks her book out of her backpack and sticks her nose in it.

I try to grin at Vee, but she looks worried. Jessie's lower lip is **trembling,** and I don't think she's really reading. She doesn't turn a page the whole way to school.

I'm in the grade below my stepsisters, so I don't see them all morning. At lunch, Vee pulls away from the older kids. She comes over to me and hisses, "We just have to let Jessie help with the car."

"Fine," I snap, "but you have to make sure your **spying** twin doesn't discover our secret."

"Fine," Vee says.

My friends are watching, and they seem shocked by the way I'm talking to Vee. Until Dad and Alice got together, Jessie and Vee were just big kids at school who I never would have talked to. Now Vee and I are sharing a secret.

I'm halfway down the hall with the vacuum cleaner when I remember we need the extension cord. Vee runs back to get it. **Jessie-the-spy** says we should get a bucket and a cloth.

"Vee!" I yell. "Get a bucket!"

Vee holds the door open with her foot and shouts back, "Did you get a trash bag already?"

"No! Can you grab one?"

Next to us, the door opens. "Will you kids shut up?" Mr. Hinkenbushel shouts.

He's so close that his voice scares me. I drop the vacuum cleaner. He stands and glares at me as I grab the handle. The girls and I drag our cleaning things to the elevator. Just when I think we're in the clear, the extension cord gets caught in the door! I yank on the cord as the doors re-open. I can feel him standing there, and I look up through my curls to see Mr. Hinkenbushel smiling meanly.

Finally the elevator doors shut, and we start to move down toward the garage. "I hate him," Jessie says.

I nod. "Me too."

We all stand there, **hating** Mr. Hinkenbushel.

Once we start, cleaning the car is actually kind of fun, and I forget Jessie is there to spy on us. Vee finds four dollars and promises to share. I find my old **ninja** sticker book. Jessie puts the little end on the vacuum cleaner and gets into all the corners. While she's got her head down, I do a quick run to the storage room with the sandwich for John.

Tappety-tap-tap-tap.

As soon as he opens the door, I shove the sandwich into his hand. "Can't stay," I say. "See you at midnight."

Chapter Five

When the elevator doors open on our floor, it's chaos. Mr. Hinkenbushel is shouting at Alice, and Alice is clutching Baby and shouting right back at Mr. Hinkenbushel. Which is weird because Alice never shouts. Baby is screaming, and Dad is trying to get everybody to calm down. He's hopping around from one foot to the other like a **gigantic crazy frog**.

"It's rude!" Mr. Hinkenbushel yells. "What they need is boundaries, and you are clearly useless at providing —"

"How dare you judge my family!" says Alice. She is pale with **fury**.

"Now, Alice," says Dad, but then he turns to the other problem. "Now, Mr. Hinkenbushel . . ." **(Hop, hop, hop.)**

They all stop like naughty children when they see us. Except Baby, who is still crying.

Alice coughs, trying not to look too crazy in front of us. Her voice turns cold and hard. "Thank you for letting us know, Mr. Hinkenbushel. Tom and I will have a *respectful* conversation with the children." She turns on her heel and bounces Baby into the kitchen.

Vee leans into me as we drag the vacuum cleaner inside, whispering, "But we were being *good*. We were cleaning the car."

"That's it," Alice announces, throwing herself down on the couch. "I'm not cooking! If everyone thinks I'm a bad mom, I'll just be a bad mom!"

Dad gives her a **shoulder squeeze** and whispers something in her ear. She laughs, gets a big fat tear in each eye, and then gives her head a shake. "Someone call that Indian food take-out place we like," she says.

When the food arrives, the roti bread is nothing like Mom's, but I don't complain. Dad **winks** at me over the lentil dish called dal, and I try to smile back. I even manage to shove some of the roti into my pocket for John Smith. Alice and Dad don't talk to us about Mr. Hinkenbushel, but they're both very quiet. It's weird. Even Baby just sits there, smearing the yogurt-like raita on a patch of table. Usually at dinner, someone is talking — even if the twins are both mad at me.

Vee does her homework without being asked, for the first time *ever*. I go and lean over her shoulder. "I think only one of us should go down tonight. It'd suck to get caught."

Vee bites her pen and nods.

I say, "I'll go tonight because I found him. You can go tomorrow night."

She turns around to argue with me, but I widen my eyes warningly. "We can't argue now!" I whisper. I know I'm being **dramatic**. But I'm kind of right too. Alice and Dad are still all weird and tense, and if we argue, they'll want to know why.

I grab the iPad before Jessie can. I hop into my bed and start up a Skype call to Mom.

Mom's working in her office and she looks busy, but she smiles at me anyway. "Hi, Squishy."

"Hi, Mom."

"How was your dinner?"

"We had Indian food, with **cardboard roti**. She laughs because "cardboard roti" is her phrase.

"It was because Mr. Hinkenbushel yelled at Alice," I add.

Mom frowns. "Your cranky next-door neighbor? Well, I don't imagine Alice took that lying down."

I grin. "She didn't. She yelled right back at him."

Mom does her funny sideways smile. "Well, I'll say this for Tom, he's got good taste." She's complimenting herself and Alice more than Dad. Mom thinks Dad is pretty annoying — so annoying that she had to break up with him and get a divorce back when I was little. But she was happy when he found Alice, a woman who is **smart** and **strong**. Mom likes Alice.

Then I think about the tears in Alice's eyes tonight.

"She said she was a bad mom," I say.

"Well, that's a crazy thing for her to say," Mom says. It's the exact same tone she uses on me when I tell her I can't do something, like she's half-irritated and half-supportive.

There's a pause.

I ask, "If I wanted to, could I come to Geneva and live with you?"

Mom shifts her arms and leans in toward the screen. "Sweetheart. Of course you can, if that's what you want. But we did talk about it a lot."

We did. I wanted to stay at my school. And Mom will be home in seven months and one week.

After goodnight kisses, I lie in my bunk in the dark, thinking about how **cranky** Mr. Hinkenbushel was and how horrible it is when he shouts.

"We should get back at him," I say. I don't need to tell Jessie and Vee who I'm talking about.

"I can't believe he shouted because we *washed the car*," Vee says.

I know that's not really why he shouted. But anyway, it's not fair.

"Did you see Mom's face?" Jessie asks.

The bunk creaks, and I can tell they are both rolling over, thinking about Mr. Hinkenbushel's **mean shouty voice** and their mom's tears.

"We should do something to make him wish he hadn't shouted," I say.

"Make him wish he'd never been born," Vee agrees.

"Revenge on our enemies," Jessie says. She likes big words.

"The Hinkenbushel Revenge Club," I say.

Vee does a **rolling-spin-drop** down to my bunk. "Come on." She drops again to Jessie. I follow down the ladder. I want to try Vee's bunk-bed move but not in the dark when we're trying to be quiet.

We are all together on Jessie's bunk.

"Let's pinkie swear," Vee says. (I think she's inspired by swearing to protect John Smith.)

"Yes, pinkie swear," Jessie says, and we knock shoulders and elbows as we hook our pinkie fingers together.

"What should we swear?" I ask.

"To get back at Mr. Hinkenbushel for yelling at us and Mom, and to keep the club a secret forever and ever."

"I swear," I say.

"I swear," says Vee.

"I swear," says Jessie. Then we do a hand wriggle, and Jessie says in a TV announcer voice, "Boom! We are the Hinkenbushel Revenge Club!"

We all burst out laughing. It's funny how her announcer voice actually makes us feel like a team.

"Kids!" Alice calls from the family room. "It's way past bedtime."

We scramble to our own bunks and lie in bed, silent for a while. I'm thinking about how much fun Jessie has been tonight. Then I remember John Smith. If we told Jessie about him, maybe it would be *more* of an adventure.

Jessie whispers, "We could leave things on Mr. Hinkenbushel's doorstep so he trips over them."

"We could sneak up behind him and stick **kick me** notes on his back," I suggest with a giggle in my throat.

"We could throw rotten fruit from our balcony to his balcony," Vee says, and we are all laughing again.

"Kids!" Alice shouts.

We're snorting into our pillows, and I'm so happy, lying in the dark, laughing and trying to be quiet. For the first time ever, I think maybe my stepsisters *are* actually kind of a bonus.

I wait again until everyone is asleep and then tiptoe down to John Smith. As I press the elevator button to get down to the garage, I start to wonder for the first time how John Smith got in that storage room. The front door needs a key card, and the garage door needs a remote.

The roti bread got kind of **smooshed** when I was lying on it, talking with Mom. But John looks pretty happy to eat something.

"How did you get in here?" I ask. "Did you run in behind a car when the door went up?"

"I'll show you," he grins.

He leads me down to the other end of the garage, where a little grate near the roof looks out at the sidewalk. He stands on the hood of the car in apartment 503's spot and reaches up to jiggle the grate. It pulls off in his hands. Then he hauls himself up through the hole. It looks a little hard, but I think I can do it.

I slither up through the hole, out onto the street.

"This," he gestures grandly, "is my own personal bathroom."

The old green public porta-potty is right opposite the grate.

"Aren't your parents worried about you?" I ask, suddenly worried about him myself. He can't hide here forever.

"They don't care," he mutters.

"They won't put you in jail," I say. "Not for borrowing a motorcycle."

"It'll be worse than jail," John says.

I don't know how to answer that, so I just stand there for a bit.

"Vee and I are bringing you gummy worms tomorrow," I say. "It's Saturday. Allowance Day."

I'm thinking hard. I bet his parents *are* worried. And I bet they don't want him to go to jail either. I need to find a way to talk it over with Vee.

Chapter Six

"Can I come to rock climbing?" I ask, dipping **toast** into my egg.

Everyone stares at me. I never want to go rock climbing because Saturday is Dad Day. But talking to Vee feels more important.

"Are you sure, sweetheart?" Dad asks.

I nod. It's perfect. Jessie will be at her violin lesson. I'm sure we can find a minute or two away from Alice.

Only problem is that the last time Alice suggested I come, Vee scowled. Later I found used teabags in my shoes. I swallow, waiting for her to say no.

"You'll need to tie back your hair," Vee says.

I grin.

After breakfast Vee tries to help me pull the **masses of curls** up into a knotty ponytail. My hair springs around everywhere, and we both start laughing. No one knows how to deal with my hair, except Mom.

I suddenly realize Jessie is doing **cross-eyes** at me again. I think she might hate it when I hang out with her twin. It gives me a mini sense of triumph.

We catch the bus together to Rockers, the rock climbing center, and Alice signs a piece of paper about me at the front desk.

"The **death form**," Vee whispers in a **fake-scary** voice.

Vee helps me into the harness, and then Alice checks it's all OK. The walls are really, really high, with little plastic knobbly bumps in different colors going all the way to the top. There are tons of other people along the wall at different heights, like flies.

I realize this was a fairly **drastic** plan for a way to talk to Vee.

Vee climbs first, and Alice shows me how to hold the rope to make sure she doesn't fall. She points out that Vee is using only one color of knobbly bumps. "They're different levels of difficulty."

I stare up at Vee. She's barely holding onto the wall with her fingertips! How can someone's fingers be so strong? She climbs higher and higher — almost to the ceiling.

By the time it's my turn I'm feeling **jittery**. What if I fall?

"I've got you," Alice says, tugging the rope so it almost lifts me at the waist. I laugh, but it's a scared kind of laugh. I wonder if Vee can tell.

I start climbing. It's easy. My fingertips hold tight to the grips, and I just clamber up, up, up. Looking for each new grip is fun, and it's satisfying to feel my arms spread wide across the wall.

"I'm like a **ninja**!" I call, looking down. Really bad move.

Alice and Vee are tiny. It's a long way to the floor.

What am I doing here? Why did I come? I don't even care about John or talking with Vee. I just care about not dying.

I'm frozen. My ears are buzzing. I realize that Vee and Alice are calling to me, but I block them out. I just grip the wall and don't let go. My hands hurt. I need to pee.

The next thing I know, Vee is on the wall next to me. **"Freaking out yet?"** She grins.

And suddenly the world feels normal again. "Not much," I say.

"Let go of the wall," she says. "Mom can lower you down."

Letting go feels like a really bad plan, but Alice gives me an encouraging tug on my harness. I grit my teeth and loosen my fingers. I swing into the air, but I don't fall — I stay right there. The harness feels a little bit like a hug.

"If you hold this rope, you can lower yourself down," Vee says. She shows me how to kick out from the wall and drift toward the ground. It's really fun. For some reason, having control feels safer than letting Alice do it.

"Can I go again?" I ask as my feet hit the floor.

Alice laughs. "Take a break," she says.

We watch Vee climb, and then it's my turn again. This time climbing doesn't feel quite so easy, but I also don't freeze when I get to the top.

By the time it's over, my arms hurt and my fingers hurt, but I have a new favorite thing. I also realize that I've totally forgotten to talk with Vee about John.

Luckily, Alice makes it easy. She grins at us. "How about this for a plan: you two catch the bus home, and I'll meet you there with lunch."

"Really?" Vee asks.

"Yep. That'll give me a climb to myself and a **catch-up** hour in the office. You'll be fine. You catch the bus to school without me, right?"

This is true. But Jessie is usually with us, and she's the responsible one.

I guess Alice thinks we're responsible enough without Jessie. And anyway, Jessie isn't *always* responsible. I think about her squeaky, **snorting** laugh into her pillow after we'd been told to be quiet.

Soon we head out to the bus stop and step onto the bus. The bus door closes, and I've got Vee to myself.

"Do you think we should tell Jessie about John?" I ask.

Chapter Seven

I press G for "garage" on the elevator
button, which means we aren't going to
the park, and Jessie notices right away.

"Where are we going?" she asks.

"We'll show you," Vee grins. It's after
lunch. We're taking Baby for his nap in
the stroller. He likes **walking-naps**,
and he's already asleep by the time we
get to the elevator, so this is going to
be easy.

"What are we doing? Is it the HRC?" Jessie asks.

"What?" Vee doesn't get it.

"Hinkenbushel Revenge Club," I say to Vee. Then to Jessie, I add, "No, it's not that. It's something just as important."

We already checked with John on our way in, and he said we could tell Jessie.

When we reach the garage, Vee is about to head for the storage room, but the scowly man from the bus stop is here. I grip Vee's arm. "Hang on a sec," I say.

We watch as the man gets in the car from apartment 503 — the car under John's secret exit. That would be why the man looked familiar at the bus stop. I must have seen him in the elevator. As he pulls out, I glimpse John's footprint on his car hood. It makes me smile. The garage door beeps down.

"All clear," I say.

Vee pulls Jessie and I push Baby over to John Smith's door. I knock my special **tappety-tap-tap-tap**.

When John opens it, Jessie stares at him. He suddenly seems shorter when face-to-face with Jessie (which is weird because she's the same height as Vee). He looks a bit frightened.

"Who are you?" Jessie asks.

"His name's John Smith. He stole a motorcycle, and now he's hiding from the police," I say quickly.

"We're protecting him with our lives," Vee explains.

The elevator dings, announcing that someone else is arriving in the garage. We tumble into the storage room before anyone sees us. Vee bumps the stroller on the door, but Baby stays asleep.

"Your name's not John Smith," Jessie pronounces.

The boy goes even whiter. "How did you know?" he stutters.

"I know *now*," Jessie says smugly.

We all stare at her. I realize she tricked him by **pretending** to know.

"Why did you choose John Smith anyway?" Jessie asks. "It's the most obvious fake name in history."

"Is it?" Not-John-Smith asks. "I saw it on a TV show, and I thought it was a good fake name."

I'm a little bit angry. "You lied! We brought you so much food, and you lied to us." I glare at him and Jessie. I'm annoyed that Jessie figured it out so quickly and I didn't.

"I bet you didn't even steal a motorcycle either," I say.

"Yeah!" Vee chimes in.

I'm just saying it because I want to make him feel bad. But his eyes go wide, and I realize *that* was a lie too.

"You didn't steal a motorcycle," I say. "You totally lied to us!"

He's biting his lip. "I saw a story about it on the news. A boy did it, and I wished it was me."

I can tell Jessie feels sorry for him. "It's part of the job of runaways to lie," Jessie says. "They have to hide the real story to protect themselves. I bet the real story's even worse, isn't it?"

Not-John-Smith is looking teary and trying not to. Worse than stealing a motorcycle and hiding from the police?

"What's your name then, Not-John?" I ask.

"If I tell you, you'll Google me," he says.

Jessie grins, and I realize she's probably going to Google him anyway.

"Not-John is a good name," I say.

Vee pulls the **gummy worms** from on top of Baby. Baby makes a cute noise and stays asleep.

"Why is there a baby?" Not-John asks.

"We stole him from a guy on a motorcycle," Vee says, and we all giggle.

There's something about the sound of the gummy worms package opening that makes me feel happy inside. We sit on the floor with the stroller between us. Jessie passes the gummy worms across the wheels to each of us.

"It's because of my dad," Not-John says, biting the head off a **green** worm. "We had a fight . . ."

He looks angry and sad at the same time, and his face nearly reminds me of something, but I'm not sure what.

"I want him to know I'm serious," Not-John says. He looks serious.

"But you can't stay here forever," Jessie says.

"Why not?" asks Not-John. "I've got a bathroom." He waves vaguely in the direction of the porta-potty. "Squishy Taylor feeds me. What's the problem?"

I imagine Not-John growing up, shaving in the porta-potty, and climbing out through the grate to go to work every morning. I suddenly think of something.

"How did you even know to come here?" I ask. "How did you know about the vent and the storage room?"

Not-John looks down at his feet.

Jessie's mouth twitches. "Did you run away from home to your own parking garage?" she asks.

Not-John doesn't say anything.

"You totally did!" Jessie says, sounding pleased with herself.

Baby rolls over, and the stroller squeaks.

I have a tingling feeling of dread and excitement. I bet I know who Not-John's dad is. I bet his dad is Mr. Hinkenbushel.

Baby starts to cry.

"Your dad," I start to say. "Is he —"

Baby's wails get louder.

"Come on, Squishy," Jessie says.

"But, Not-John's dad —"

"Squishy, we have to get out of here. The next person who comes into the garage is going to hear screaming and wonder who's chained up in the storage room."

I stare at Jessie. She's right. And she's made me think of something.

"OK," I say as she pulls me out the door.

Chapter Eight

"There's absolutely, one hundred percent, no way his dad is Mr. Hinkenbushel," Jessie says. "That would mean we haven't noticed that there's a kid living right next door to us. For years. No way."

We are pushing the stroller to the playground. It's not time for Baby's nap to finish yet. He likes the feel of the stroller wheels rolling, and he's already closed his eyes again.

"But what if," I say excitedly, "what if that's exactly why he ran away? What if Mr. Hinkenbushel keeps him **chained up** in the closet?"

Vee looks nervous, but Jessie snorts. "He's got a backpack. And a sunburn."

"But Mr. Hinkenbushel is so mean. That's exactly what he would do. It's probably why he's even meaner this week. Because his prisoner got away. And maybe it's not a sunburn, maybe it's a **skin disease**."

Vee giggles, and even I realize that's a little silly.

"Well, whether or not Mr. Hinkenbushel is his dad, we have to get revenge," I say.

Jessie nods. "He still hates us, and he shouted at Mom."

At the playground, Vee and I push the stroller over to the monkey bars. Jessie goes to sit on the bench next to another girl from school who's got an iPad.

I show Vee my new monkey bar moves. During one really cool trick, I swing **upside-down** from my knees and brush the stroller with my hair. It's hard, because if you get it wrong, you either don't touch the stroller or you bash your face on it.

Vee's impressed. "You should do some bunk-bed tricks with me," she says.

"OK," I say, a bit surprised because of how much she hated me doing the same **bunk-bed acrobatics** before.

Baby wakes up screaming, and we have to run to get him home. Well, not run exactly, because we aren't allowed to run with Baby when we're next to the road. We just walk really, really fast. Kind of jog-walk.

As we get closer to home, we pass a huge dog out for a walk. I see the owner clutching a swinging plastic bag with a **squooshy-looking** weight in the bottom of it. And I have the best Hinkenbushel Revenge Club idea ever.

"Wait a sec," I say as we pull up to our apartment building's front door.

I follow the huge dog and its owner until they reach the trash can at the corner. As I suspected, the owner leaves the **squooshy** plastic bag in the trash and keeps walking.

I hang around the trash can until the traffic lights change and the big dog crosses the road. Then I **snatch** the bag from the can and run back to where Jessie and Vee are waiting for me. I wave the bag like a trophy. "It's for the HRC!" I yell.

Vee and Jessie whoop and laugh.

When we get in the elevator, the familiar scowly man is there too. Somehow, he's even more scowly than before. He looks at us and the stroller, and the look in his eyes makes me wonder if he's not angry, actually just sad. The doors open on the fifth floor, and I watch him get out.

When the doors close again, the twins **collapse** with laughter. Vee is clinging to the stroller, flopping over the side. Baby grabs Vee's hair, and when she stands up, it makes him sit up. Then we laugh even harder and nearly forget to leave the elevator.

But as soon as we do, I shush them. Mr. Hinkenbushel's door is closed. Now's the time, before he comes home.

I crouch by Mr. Hinkenbushel's doormat and dump the contents of the bag onto it.

"This is for you, Alice," I whisper.

Wow. That was a **big dog**. Everything that dog did was big. I stare at the mound on Mr. Hinkenbushel's doormat and then quickly stand up and back away. **Disgusting**. We pile into our place, giggling.

The HRC has made its first move.

Chapter Nine

I **roll** from the top bunk . . .

Grab the rail with one hand . . . **Swing** and **kick** my feet out horizontally —

and then **land**, standing, on the desk.

I have to steady myself against the wall, but Vee claps anyway from the top bunk. "Awesome!" she says.

The whole bunk is still creaking and the telescope is rattling on its legs.

"Can you show me the next move?" I ask, jumping down to the floor.

Vee follows me to the desk, but she doesn't stop there. She grabs the top of the cabinet, **secret-agent-rolls** across it only inches from the ceiling, and then kicks off the wall, returning to lying down flat on her bunk. The bed shakes wildly, and I clap.

Jessie looks up from where she's been reading the iPad on her bunk. "There are no boys reported missing from this area in the last week," she says. "At least none who are Not-John's age."

That stops Vee and me in our tracks.

"It must be Mr. Hinkenbushel," I say. "He can't report it, because then they'll know he's been keeping prisoners."

Jessie looks doubtful, but I'm starting to wonder if I might be right.

"I wonder if he's **stepped** in it yet," Vee says, and we all shriek with laughter. Vee does a **quick-drop** to the floor and a **kicking-two-jump-scramble** back to her bunk. The dresser booms hard against the wall. A moment later, Alice appears in the doorway.

"Enough!" she says. "I take you rock climbing to burn off energy so I don't have to put up with these stunts at home.

Can't you do something quiet for a while? Maybe you can all do a project together on the iPad?"

We spend the time before dinner making an HRC website on the iPad. Jessie works the iPad while Vee and I help by listing Mr. Hinkenbushel's **crimes** and all the ways we're going to get back at him.

While Jessie is doing the complicated work, Vee and I take turns looking through the telescope at the boring people in the offices across the road. When the website is pretty much finished, we make a YouTube clip of us **"declaring revenge,"** as Jessie puts it. It's awesome.

"Dinner!" Dad calls. We tumble into the kitchen. "Tonight it's roll-your-own rice-paper rolls."

The table is covered with lots of bowls of things cut up small. I pile my first roll with pork and sauce. Yum. I add a little bit of carrot when Alice does an **eat-your-vegetables face** at me. There's too much pork and the whole thing falls apart, but I don't care.

I pick pieces up with my fingers and smear them around the sauce on my plate. Alice seems to have gotten over being shouted at yesterday, and dinnertime is back to normal. Except in the old normal, Jessie and Vee weren't this nice to me.

"Is it movie night?" I ask.

Jessie is halfway through a neat roll. "Can we download something new, pleeeease?" she asks.

"Ba-ba-ba," says Baby, slamming a plate of cucumber sticks to the floor. We all laugh, including Baby, and I jump down to pick them up.

"Ten-second rule!" I shout as I gather the cucumber pieces together. It's not until I stand up again that I see there's something white on the floor in front of the door. "Hey, what's that?"

"What's what?" asks Dad.

"It's a piece of paper," I say, going over to the door. "That's weird."

We never get paper under our door. Letters come to the mailbox downstairs in the lobby.

"Give it here," Dad says, reaching for it, but not before I get a glimpse of the picture. It's Not-John, with **"MISSING"** written in big letters across the top.

My heart slams into double-speed. I try to see over Dad's shoulder, but my eyes are jumping around, trying to read everything at once and not getting anything at all.

"There's a boy missing from the building," Dad says.

Alice gasps and grabs her mouth. I don't think I've ever seen a grown-up look so scared.

"Apparently he left a note, and he's been texting his dad and pretending he's at his grandmother's." Dad looks up at Alice. "Sounds more like a runaway than a kidnapping."

Alice's hand drops away from her mouth. She looks a bit relieved but not much.

Dad keeps reading. Jessie and Vee and I can't help staring at each other.

"The note is from the boy's father, who only realized his son was missing when he talked to the grandmother . . ." Dad checks the clock, ". . . an hour ago. But he's been gone for three days."

"Three days?" Alice looks like she's going to cry. She grips Vee's hand.

"He wants to know if anyone has seen his son." Dad puts the note on the table.

None of us feel like eating.

"The poor man. He must be terrified," Alice says, pushing back her chair and taking the note. "I'm going to stop over and visit him right away."

As soon as she opens the door, the whole apartment begins to smell of dog poop.

Chapter Ten

"We have to tell them," Jessie hisses. We're loading the dishwasher and putting leftovers in the fridge. Dad is in the other room talking on the phone. Baby is sitting on the floor between us, **dribbling** chewed cucumber. The kitchen stinks, and I'm seriously regretting our first HRC revenge attack.

"We can't keep Not-John a secret anymore," Jessie whispers.

"But we promised!" I say. I remember staring into Not-John's eyes and swearing not to tell.

Vee looks torn. A promise is a promise. "But if the dad is half as terrified as Alice was —" she starts.

"But what if we're right? What if his dad *is* Mr. Hinkenbushel? What if we need to protect him from his dad?" I say. I know I might be wrong. But I might also be right. "We can't deliver him into the hands of his enemy."

"Squishy, this is serious! Stop being ridiculous," Jessie says in her most horrible grown-up tone.

I was serious. It just came out a bit dramatic. I glare at her. "I'm not being ridiculous!

You're being a **know-it-all goody-goody**."

Jessie comes over toward me but accidentally kicks Baby in the shoulder. Baby falls over onto one fat cheek and starts wailing.

"Look what you did to my brother!" I say as I step forward to pick him up.

"*Your* brother? He's *our* brother!" Vee says.

We all bend down, racing to pick him up first.

Bang! All three of our foreheads knock together. "Ouch!" we all shout.

Jessie picks up Baby and stands shoulder to shoulder with Vee. They glare at me with **matching twin glares**.

"Fine!" I yell. "Have him! I don't even care. I don't even want him. Not if I

have to live with evil twinsies. And your horrible mom. I don't want *any* of you."

My stomach lurches, like something awful just happened. I wish I was in Geneva with Mom. I wish Mom never went to Geneva in the first place. I wish I could take back what I said and still be friends with Jessie and Vee. But I can't.

"What's going on, girls?" Dad comes over, holding the phone away from his ear. "Good grief, what's that smell?"

Vee is still clutching her forehead. **"It's doggie-doo,"** she says. "Squishy left it on Mr. Hinkenbushel's doormat, and now it's everywhere."

"You did *what?!*"

Baby struggles in Jessie's arms, crying. Dad is staring at me in horror. I am staring at Vee, feeling huge waves of **betrayal** roll over me. Also, my head is pounding where we knocked together.

"It was revenge!" I half-sob, half-shout. "I did it because of how he yelled at your mom! You guys thought it was **funny**," I plead, glancing at Jessie and Vee. Jessie still looks furious, but Vee is white. She looks like I feel.

"Dad . . . ?" But I don't know what to say next. Which is weird.

Dad looks at me for a long moment. I think I see a kind of understanding in his eyes. There's a tinny voice coming out of his phone, and finally he puts it to his ear. "Sorry, I'm going to have to call you back."

"There's something else too," Jessie starts in her **know-it-all** voice. She's going to tell about Not-John.

"Not now, Jessie," Dad says, taking Baby.

"But —" Jessie starts.

"Not —" Dad says.

"It's about —" Jessie tries again.

"Jessie, this is *not* the time."

I've never heard Dad use that tone with anyone except me. It shocks me. It's like being in a whole different world where I actually have a sister.

"Right now, I need to talk with Sita. Alone." Dad only calls me Sita when things are really serious. He turns and walks into his and Alice's room.

I stare at Jessie, feeling sick. Vee told on me, and I said something horrible.

And now Jessie wants to tell on Not-John. I'm thinking of Not-John's white face. He said whatever was waiting for him was **worse than jail**. We can't break the promise we made him.

"Please, please don't tell yet," I whisper. "We promised." I look at Vee, remembering the promise we made, and she looks undecided. But Jessie is stony. I try to bargain. "'Give me one hour. If it's not sorted out in an hour, I'll tell them about it myself."

"Sita!" Dad calls in the kind of voice you can't ignore.

"Please?" I beg.

Vee turns to Jessie. She's asking Jessie to wait too, with her eyes.

"Half an hour," Jessie says grimly.

I turn and run in to Dad.

He says all the things. About how it was bad for Mr. Hinkenbushel to shout at Alice, but that didn't mean it was OK to put dog poop on his doormat. About how he knows I must want to do funny things to make Jessie and Vee like me. About how he's glad I like Alice enough to want to protect her, but that she's quite capable of protecting herself.

"You know, Squisho, those two aren't just stepsisters."

I can hear the **"bonus sisters"** talk coming, and I bite my lip and nod, thinking about how I just said Alice was horrible and that I didn't want Baby. I hate being lectured when people are actually serious. Both Mom and Dad are a little bit proud when I'm a **rebel** — I can hear it in their voices. But Dad doesn't think anything is funny right now. And he won't stop talking. Every minute he keeps going is a minute less for me to get to Not-John and warn him to run away or convince him to turn himself in.

"Are we clear?" Dad asks finally.

I nod.

"Look at me, Sita," he says. I look up into his eyes. "I love you," he says and pulls me into a hug.

"Dad . . . ?" I start to say with my mouth pressed into his shoulder.

"Yeah, Squisho . . . ?"

"Can I run down and grab my silver sweater? I think I left it in the car."

"Um. Sure." He sounds a bit surprised, but he lets me go.

I dash out into the kitchen. "I'm going down to grab my silver sweater out of the car," I say to Jessie and Vee, doing air quotes, hoping they'll understand what I mean. I **bolt** out into the stinking hall. The clock is ticking.

Chapter Eleven

I know it's probably faster to take the elevator, but I can't bear to stand still. I pound down the stairs. The stairwell **stinks** for at least the first four floors. Has someone walked with dog poop on their shoe down every single hall? Then I realize: of course someone did. Not-John's dad with the "missing" notice.

This is another piece of evidence that Mr. Hinkenbushel is Not-John's dad.

What am I going to do if he is? I can't turn Not-John in to his dad if his dad is that horrible.

When I reach the bottom of the stairs, the garage is creepy as ever, but I don't care anymore. There's nobody else here. I **race** between the cars to Not-John's door and knock, forgetting any secret code.

He looks happy to see me until he realizes I didn't bring any food.

"Why did you run away?" I ask.

"Because I . . . my dad . . . he just . . . What's that **smell**?"

"Is your dad Mr. Hinkenbushel? Did you run away because he chained you in a closet your whole life?"

"Um . . . what are you talking about?" Not-John is staring at me like I'm crazy.

"OK fine, I was wrong." I'm almost disappointed, but then I realize it's a good thing Not-John's dad isn't that mean. "So why did you say it will be worse than jail?"

"It's a **stepmom**!" he wails. "My dad's got a new girlfriend, and we're going to move in with her, and my life is **OVER**."

I just keep staring at him.

"What?" he asks. "What's wrong?"

"You want me to protect you with my life against your **stepmom**?"

"Well, I didn't actually ask —"

"Have you met *my* stepfamily?" I interrupt.

"Well, yes . . . but that's different. You've lived together forever, and you never fight," Not-John says.

I laugh. "Are you kidding?"

I think about the **horrible** thing I just said to my stepsisters and how Vee betrayed me. But I realize those things aren't even that important. "You have to talk to your dad," I say. "He's talked to your grandma. The police are looking for you and so is everyone in this building."

Not-John turns pale and looks around the storage room. "I need to get out of here."

"Maybe you should talk to your dad," I say.

"He doesn't care."

Not-John starts shoving things into his backpack. This was not the plan. If he runs away where we can't protect him, **anything** might happen. I think about his dad, who must be really worried.

I remember how scared Alice looked when she heard a child was missing from the building. Not-John's father must be a **million** times more scared than that. I suddenly think how sad Mom was when I decided not to go to Geneva and how much I love her. It gives me an idea.

"OK, OK," I say. "New plan. You get your backpack. Wait by the grate. I'll go outside and signal when it's safe to leave." I pause, making things up. "Um, there's three policemen out there, so you'll have to wait for me to distract them, and listen carefully for my signal."

Not-John nods seriously.

I **bolt** to the elevator.

"Dad, call Alice," I say, as I burst into the kitchen.

"What? Why?" Dad asks, turning toward me from where he is sitting with the twins. Jessie is sitting upright, and Vee is sprawled back on her chair. They both look **sulky**, like Dad has been talking seriously with them too.

"Quick," I say. "This is important."

"But you said —"

"Dad! Call her!"

He starts rummaging for his phone.

I gesture at Jessie and Vee, pointing downward and making a big anxious face, trying to make them understand how important this is.

Dad has found his phone, but he still isn't dialing. He's sitting there, looking at me. **He's so hopeless.**

"Did Alice take her phone?" he asks.

The twins say together, "She always takes her phone!" and I can tell they are on my side, at least for now.

"What do I say?" he asks.

"Argh!" I snatch the phone and call her myself. "Alice, are you still with Not-Jo — the boy's dad? Yes? OK, meet us outside of the building in seven minutes. Bring him. It's important." Everyone is staring at me. "Come on!" I say, as I push the phone back at Dad. "There's no time!"

We all run out the door. Vee picks up Baby from the rug, and Jessie takes the key. Dad just flutters his arms around, asking, "What? Who? Why?" and follows behind us.

Chapter Twelve

It's dark outside, which I had forgotten
about, but luckily there's a streetlight
just where I need it. I lead the way to the
sidewalk near Not-John's secret grate.
Then I stand right in front of it. I've got
about five minutes before Alice shows
up with Not-John's dad. Hopefully I can
swing this before then.

"Um, while we wait, Jessie and Vee, I
have to . . . um . . . apologize."

I truly hope this works because it's **really, really embarrassing**.

"I'm sorry I said you were evil and I didn't want any of you. Really sorry. It's not true."

As I'm speaking, I realize I'm not just doing this to trick Not-John. I'm apologizing because I've wanted to ever since the mean words burst out of me.

"I still really wish you weren't such a **know-it-all** about everything," I say to Jessie. But I say it in a light, teasing way.

"Can't help being smart," she replies.

We look at each other and kind of smile a little.

I turn to Vee. "And I'm still mad at you for laughing while I did the dog poop and then telling on me like that." Then I grin. "But, turns out it was a **stinky** idea."

Vee cracks a smile. "Well, telling on people kind of **reeks**," she says, and now we're all laughing except Dad, who's just standing there, holding Baby and looking a bit confused about why we're out on the street.

"And you know what?" I say to my stepsisters. "You *are* a bonus. You're a **crazy-awesome bonus**." I'm thinking about laughing in the elevator and whispering late at night until we have to snort into our pillows. I'm thinking about Vee teaching me all of her **bunk-bed tricks** and Jessie making us all pinkie swear to join the HRC.

I take a deep breath. "So I'm not going to call you stepsisters anymore. From now on, you are my bonus sisters."

It's just as cheesy as I thought, but no one is looking at me like I'm an idiot. Jessie hugs me, and Vee wraps her arms around from the other side.

I'm squished in between them, and it's **perfect**.

"What is going on?" Alice asks.

We pull apart. Alice walks up to us with the tall, scowly man in the neat blue coat. Except he's not wearing a coat today, he's wearing a brown sweater.

I realize right away why I always thought he looked familiar. He looks like Not-John. And he's got the same sad-angry face that Not-John has so much of the time. This guy is really not Mr. Hinkenbushel. I feel absolutely awful about keeping our secret from this poor man.

"Squishy?" Alice asks.

I look at Not-John's dad. "It's about your kid," I say. "Um . . ." I cross my fingers, hoping this will work. "How do you feel about him being gone?"

I step sideways so that when the man turns toward me, Not-John will be able to see his face from the grate.

Not-John's dad looks at me like I'm a crazy lady surrounded by a zoo. But he answers my question. "I'm . . . I . . . he . . . I'm so afraid for him, I can't actually think." His face is pale and serious with wide eyes. I was right. He looks more than just worried. He looks scared and alone.

There's a silence, and I think maybe I've failed. I'm going to have to **betray** Not-John after all.

But then the grate behind me rattles and pushes out. There is Not-John's face at sidewalk level. He struggles out onto his belly, then up and into his dad's arms.

I watch Not-John's feet kicking the air as his dad picks him up and turns him slowly around on the spot, their faces hidden in each other's shoulders.

I get a big, soft feeling of relief that they are together again.

We did it. Me and my crazy awesome **bonus sisters**.

We say goodbye to Not-John and his dad in the elevator. Not-John tells us his real name, but we don't care.

"You'll always be Not-John-Smith to us," Vee says.

When the elevator opens on our floor, Mr. Hinkenbushel is standing in the hall looking furious.

He growls, "What is this awful smell?

"I don't know," says Jessie. "It kinda smells **sweet** to me."

Dad gives her a sideways look, but I can tell he's more laughing than angry.

When the door closes, I ask, "Can we watch a movie now because it's Saturday night — please?"

"No," Dad says.

"But you said —" Jessie starts.

"It's ten at night," Dad says.

"But —" Vee says.

"Bed!" shouts Alice, and we scamper.

I do a quick **running-cross-spin-leap** into my bunk and nearly take out the telescope.

"You know," I say, once the lights are off, "I bet Mr. Hinkenbushel does keep prisoners **chained** in his closet. We just haven't discovered them yet."

About the
Author
and
Illustrator

Ailsa Wild is an acrobat, whip-cracker, and teaching artist who ran away from the circus to become a writer. She taught Squishy all her best bunk-bed tricks.

Ben Wood started drawing when he was Baby's age and happily drew all over his mom and dad's walls! Since then, he has never stopped drawing. He has an identical twin, and they used to play all kinds of pranks on their younger brother.

Author Acknowledgements

Christy and Luke, for writing residencies, bunk-bed acrobatics, and the day you turned the truck around.

Antoni, Penni, Moreno, and the masterclass crew, for showing me what the journey could be. Here's to epiphanies.

Indira and Devika, because she couldn't be real without you.

Hilary, Marisa, Penny, Sarah, and the HGE team, for making it happen. What an amazing net to have landed in.

Ben, for bringing them all to life.

Jono, for independence and supporting each other's dreams.

— Ailsa

Illustrator Acknowledgements

Hilary, Marisa, Sarah, and the HGE team, for your enthusiasm and spark.

Penny, for being the best! Thanks for inviting me along on this Squish-tastic ride! (And for putting up with all my emails!)

Ailsa, for creating such a fun place for me to play in.

John, for listening to me ramble on and on about Squishy Taylor every day.

— Ben

Talk About It!

1. What happens in the story to make Squishy and her stepsisters become bonus sisters?

2. Why doesn't Squishy tell anyone right away about Not-John hiding in the garage? What are the pros and cons of her decision?

3. Squishy, Vee, and Jessie form a club to get revenge on Mr. Hinkenbushel. Do you think it's OK to get revenge on someone? Why or why not?

Write About It!

1. Squishy is good at keeping Not-John's secret. Write about one thing that would have happened differently if Squishy had told her dad about Not-John right away.

2. Think about how Squishy, Vee, and Jessie overcame their differences in this story. Now write about how you overcame your differences with someone to become friends.

3. Why do you think Squishy's dad calls Vee and Jessie bonus sisters rather than stepsisters? Write about someone in your life who isn't related to you but feels like part of your family.